# Shopkins™
Once you shop...You can't stop!

# CORNY JOKES AND RIDDLES

SCHOLASTIC INC.

Published by Scholastic Inc., *Publishers since 1920.* SCHOLASTIC and associated logos are trademarks and/or registered trademarks of Scholastic Inc.

The publisher does not have any control over and does not assume any responsibility for author or third-party websites or their content.

This book is a work of fiction. Names, characters, places, and incidents are either the product of the author's imagination or are used fictitiously, and any resemblance to actual persons, living or dead, business establishments, events, or locales is entirely coincidental.

ISBN 978-0-545-94049-8

10 9 8 7 6 5          16 17 18 19 20

Printed in the U.S.A.          40

First printing, January 2016

# HI THERE!

I'm Corny Cob, and my Shopkins™ friends and I can't wait to share our hilarious jokes and tricky riddles with you. Just turn the page to discover a cartful of fun.

**GO ON, CHECK IT OUT!**

3

Where do
**SUPERHEROES**
go shopping?

Answer:
At the supermarket,
of course!

Why did
SPILT MILK
stop reading her
new book?

Answer:
Someone spoiled
the ending.

What type of shoes does **SLICK BREADSTICK** always wear?

Answer:
Loafers

My **FIRST** and **THIRD SYLLABLES** are the fingers of your feet.

My **SECOND SYLLABLE** is the month when flowers bloom.

Put them together to find a juicy fruit some people think is a vegetable. What am I?

_____

7

What is
**APPLE BLOSSOM'S**
signature dance move?

Answer:
The Worm

Why does
MISS MUSHY-MOO
like to throw parties?

Answer:
Because she knows
how to have fun-gus.

Which fruit's **NAME** is the same as its **COLOR**?

_____

Answer: Orange

Why is
**POSH PEAR**
such a trendsetter?

Answer:
Because her
style has appeal.

What do you
get when you cross a SHOE
with a BANANA PEEL?

Answer:
A slipper!

Is it easy to trick
**LOLLI POPPINS?**

Answer:
Nope. She's no
sucker.

My **FIRST SYLLABLE** is a dirty black lump that Santa gives to naughty children.

My **SECOND SYLLABLE** turns red and gold in autumn.

Together, my **THIRD** and **FOURTH SYLLABLES** are a beautiful bloom like a rose or daisy.

Put them together to find a white veggie that some think looks like fluffy clouds. What am I?

_____

14

Answer: Cauliflower (coal-leaf-flower)

I have a tree in my name, but I am no evergreen. I also have a fruit in my name that I am not related to at all. I am a tropical treasure, spiky on the outside, and sweet on the inside. What am I?

_____

15

I sound like the **20TH LETTER OF THE ALPHABET,** and I'm always getting into hot water. What am I?

_____

Answer: Tea

After I get **STEAMED,**
I'm very good at
**SMOOTHING**
things out.
What am I?

_____

17

I am American,
but I am also Swiss.
Sometimes I stink, and
occasionally feel blue, but I just
keep getting better with age.
What am I?

_____

Answer: Cheese

What do you get if you cross
**SODA POPS**
with
**CHEEKY CHOCOLATE?**

Answer:
Cocoa-Cola

How does
KOOKY COOKIE
win a game of basketball?

Answer:
By dunking

Why is
GOOGY
such a good teacher?

Answer:
He loves to
EGG-splain things!

Where is
**CHEE ZEE'S**
dream vacation
destination?

Answer:
The Swiss Alps

Why did

**D'LISH DONUT**

go outside in the rain?

Answer:
She likes being covered in sprinkles.

Why is
**CORNY COB**
such a good listener?

Answer:
Because
he's all ears.

What did
**SNEAKY WEDGE**
say when a fly
landed on her?

Answer:
SHOE!

Why is
**MARSHA MELLOW**
afraid of campfires?

Answer:
She's been
burned before.

My **FIRST SYLLABLE** is something you write with that's white and a little messy.

My **SECOND SYLLABLE** is something you might shout when you're surprised.

And my **THIRD SYLLABLE** is the opposite of a *little*.

Put them together to find a type of sweet treat that you should enjoy in moderation. What am I?

_____

Answer: Chocolate (chalk-oh-lot)

What is
**TACO TERRIE'S**
favorite hobby?

Answer:
Salsa dancing!

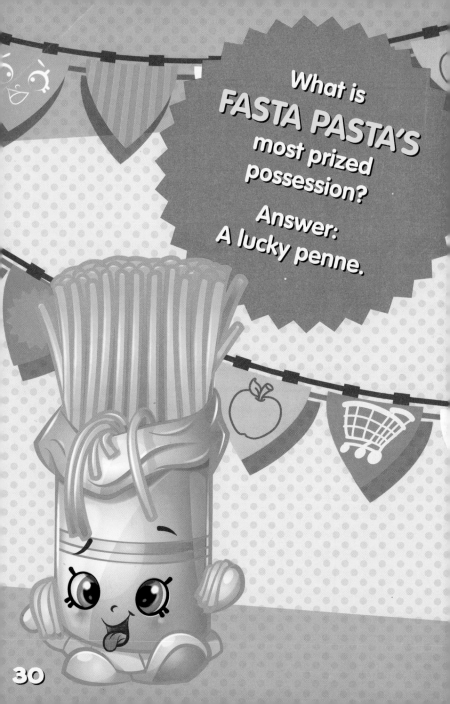

What is
FASTA PASTA'S
most prized
possession?

Answer:
A lucky penne.

30

My **FIRST SYLLABLE**
is what you do with an eraser.

My **SECOND SYLLABLE**
is a small town or ice island.

My **THIRD SYLLABLE**
is the feeling we celebrate on
Valentine's Day.

Put them
together to find a
helping hand for
washing dishes.
What am I?

_____

What primate did
MARY MERINGUE
dress up as for Halloween?

Answer:
A meringue-utan

What is
SUNNY SCREEN'S
favorite color?

Answer:
Ultraviolet

SPF
30+

I may be STRINGY, but I'm a BUCKET OF FUN. I love to clean and am at my best when I'm wet and wrung out. What am I?

_____

Answer: A mop

I love to **CELEBRATE** special occasions and am always invited to the **PARTY**.

I've got **LAYERS**, everyone thinks I'm **SWEET**, and I light up a room. What am I?

_____

Answer: Birthday cake

35

Everyone's always **BUZZING** about me. I'm sweet, but I'm not sugar. I'm golden and delicious, but I'm not an apple. And don't call me baby or sweetheart! What am I?

_____

My
**FIRST SYLLABLE**
is a game played with
a ball and glove.

My
**SECOND SYLLABLE**
is the opposite
of down.

Put them
together to find a
favorite topping
for hamburgers and
hot dogs.
What am I?

_____

38

One of us is **BLACK**, the other is **WHITE**. You will almost always find us together, shaking up a storm.

We're **SEASONED** and full of flavor, but a pinch of us goes a long way. What are we?

_____

Why did
BRENDA BLENDA
get detention?

Answer:
She was stirring up trouble.

My **FIRST SYLLABLE**
is the state you hope to leave
your doctor's office in.

My **SECOND SYLLABLE**
is found in the middle of the word *sandy*.

My **THIRD SYLLABLE**
sounds like the noise that
a ghost makes.

My **FOURTH SYLLABLE**
is a warm drink that you
enjoy with honey.

What aisle
am I?

_____

Why isn't
FREEZY PEAZY
worried about the big race?

Answer:
He already
has it in the bag.

Where did
**ICE CREAM
DREAM**
learn manners?

Answer:
Sundae school

43

My **FIRST SYLLABLE** is the sound of a bursting balloon.

My **SECOND SYLLABLE** is how you feel when you have the flu.

My **THIRD SYLLABLE** is what you make when you use the telephone.

Put them together to find an icy treat that melts in your mouth. What am I?

_____

Answer: Popsicle (pop-sick-call)

My **FIRST SYLLABLE**
is the way to eat a lollipop.

My **SECOND SYLLABLE**
is the center of an apple.

My **THIRD SYLLABLE**
can mean *about* or
*approximately.*

Put them together
to find a strong-tasting
sweet that comes in
black, red,
or rainbow.
What am I?

_____

What is
**PRETZ-ELLE'S**
favorite kind of story?

Answer:
Mysteries—she loves
anything with a twist!

Why doesn't
**BREAD HEAD**
like warm weather?

Answer:
Because things
get *toasty*!

Who is
GRAN JAM'S
hero?

Answer:
Alexander the Grape.